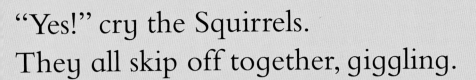

"Yes!" cry the Squirrels.
They all skip off together, giggling.

"Duggee!" call the Squirrels. "What are you doing?"
"Woof woof," says Duggee. He's collecting wood for a
campfire so they can all toast marshmallows.
"Ooooh!" gasps Tag. "Can we help collect wood, Duggee?"
"Ah-woof!" says Duggee. Of course the Squirrels can help!

The Squirrels dash off
to collect wood . . .

Happy borrows Bear's
wooden spoon.

Norrie finds a wooden peg
on Horse's washing line.

Tag grabs Gloria the pig's
wooden tennis racket.

Betty takes Alain the lion's wooden cane.

And Roly breaks off Bird's wooden door!

"We've found lots of wood, Duggee," says Norrie. "Uhh-woof? Woof!" says Duggee, looking at all the wooden objects.

You can't put just *any* wooden thing on the campfire, Squirrels. Especially things that belong to other people.

"Oh, sorry," say the Squirrels, racing to return everything.

The Squirrels hurry back to Duggee.

"So what *should* we collect for the campfire, Duggee?" asks Tag.

"Aaah-woof," says Duggee.

"Sticks?" say the Squirrels.

"What kind of sticks?" asks Betty.

Duggee knows all about sticks. He has his **Stick Badge!**

"Woof woof woof," says Duggee. The Squirrels need . . .

little sticks . . .

medium sticks . . .

and big sticks.

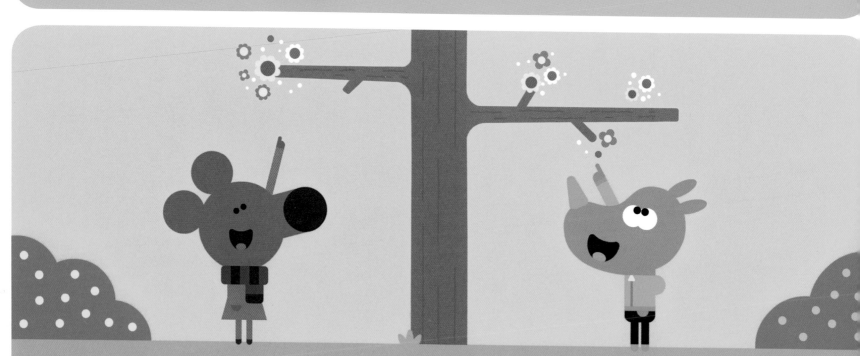

"Like these ones?" ask Norrie and Tag, pointing to some branches.
No, those ones have flowers growing on them.

"How about this one?" asks Happy, finding a stick in a puddle.
No, that one's a bit wet.

"This one?" asks Roly, hanging
off a branch with a nest on it.
No, that one's being used.

"This one?" asks Betty.
"Ah-woof!" says Duggee.
That stick is perfect, because it's
dry and lying on the ground.
"Let's find more sticks!"
say the Squirrels.

Norrie finds a stick on the ground. "YES!" she cheers.

Happy finds another stick on the ground. It's all bumpy. "YES!" cheers Happy.

Tag finds a really big log. "YES!" he cheers, rolling it over to Duggee.

Roly picks up a stick. "YEESSS!" he shouts.
Suddenly, two eyes pop open . . .

"EYES? On a stick?" gasps Roly, confused.

"Did you just . . . talk?" asks Roly.
Roly runs straight over to tell Duggee and the other Squirrels.

"Look what I've found!" cries Roly.
"Yes, Roly," says Betty. "We've all been collecting sticks."
"Not like this one," says Roly. "It's *special*."
Roly's stick leaps out of his hand and squeaks, "Stick!"
"Huh?" gasp the Squirrels.

"Woof woof woof!" says Duggee, shaking his head.
It's not a stick. It's a stick *insect*!

"But it looks like a stick," says Happy.

STICK!

"It smells like a stick," says Betty.

STICK!

"It tastes like a stick," says Roly.

STICK!

Stick looks a bit nervous.

"Ah-woof," says Duggee. If a stick insect gets scared and wants to hide, its eyes disappear and it makes itself look like a stick.
"WOW!" gasp the Squirrels.

Suddenly, Stick springs up, and his eyes pop open again.
He starts bouncing up and down, singing . . .

STICK, STICK, STICK, STICK,

STICK, STICK, STICK, STICK,

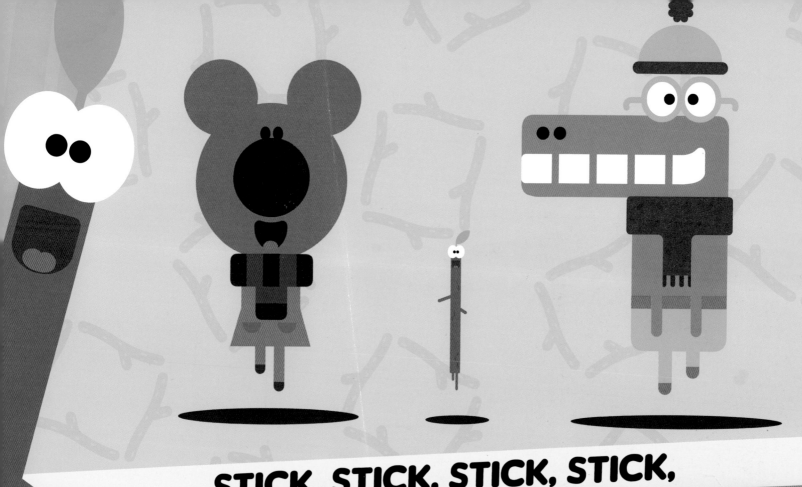

STICK, STICK, STICK, STICK,

STICKY-STICKY STICK-STICK!

STICK, STICK, STICK, STICK,

STICK, STICK, STICK, STICK,

STICK, STICK, STICK, STICK,

STICKY-STICKY STICK-STICK!

Everyone bounces and sings along until . . .

It's time for marshmallows!
The Squirrels' parents join them
around the campfire.
"We've made a new friend!" the
Squirrels tell them.
"Where is this new friend?" asks
Norrie's dad.

The Squirrels look around. Suddenly,
a pair of eyes pops open and . . .

STICK, STICK, STICK, STICK . . .

STICKY-STICKY STICK-STICK!"

"Yay!" cheer the Squirrels, bouncing
along to "The Stick Song" again.

Haven't the Squirrels done well today, Duggee? They have definitely earned their **Stick Badges**.

AH-WOOF!

Now there's just time for one last thing before
the Squirrels go home . . .